THE SMALL THINGS

LISA THOMPSON

Illustrated by
Hannah Coulson

First published in 2021 in Great Britain by
Barrington Stoke Ltd
18 Walker Street, Edinburgh, EH3 7LP

www.barringtonstoke.co.uk

A CIP catalogue record for this book is available from the British Library upon request

ISBN: 978-1-78112-964-7

Printed by Hussar Books, Poland

For Lily (and Lily-Bot)

Chapter One

It was pouring with rain on the day Ellie joined our class. On our drive to school, Mum had to put the windscreen wipers on to their fastest setting. They whizzed back and forth, but the windscreen was still blurry as we looked out into the heavy shower.

Mum pulled into a parking space close to the school gates and kept the engine running.

I didn't move.

"Come on, love, off you go," Mum said. "I've got to get to work."

I watched the streaks of rain run down my window.

"Can't we wait a little longer?" I said. "There's still ten minutes until the bell goes."

Mum sighed. "I can't, Anna," she told me. "The traffic is always bad on Mondays. I need to get Henry to nursery and I can't be late for work."

I sighed. There were three reasons why I didn't want to get out of the car.

Nia Gibson, Shavina Bates and Erin Smith.

They were all standing in the playground huddled under an umbrella.

Nia, Shavina and Erin were lovely. They weren't nasty to me in any way and I guess I'd call them my friends – even if I was on the edge of the group.

Shavina and Erin were never far from Nia and hung on to her every word. Sometimes I thought Nia was like the sun and the rest of us were planets, orbiting around her. There was nothing wrong with Nia, Shavina or Erin at all. They just made me feel so small.

"Come on, Anna," said Mum. "I'm going to be late."

My little brother kicked the back of my seat as if I needed reminding that he was there. I picked up my school bag, which was down by my feet.

"There's an umbrella in the boot," said Mum. "Take it with you or you'll get soaked. And remember we're going to the supermarket after school."

I groaned. My parents liked to go shopping later in the day when things were reduced and there were more bargains to be had. We went at least twice a week.

"Bye," I said.

I got out of the car and shut the door as the rain hit me in the face. I put my head down and trudged towards the gates. Behind me, I heard Mum shout out of the car window.

"Anna! The umbrella!" she said. I ignored her and kept walking.

I got to the playground and headed over to where Nia, Shavina and Erin sheltered under their umbrella. I stood behind them.

"It was incredible!" said Nia. "The slope was so high and it was real snow!"

Shavina and Erin gasped.

"Real snow?" said Shavina. "How can they use real snow?"

I remembered then that Nia had gone to an indoor ski slope at the weekend.

“Morning!” I said brightly. I hoped when they saw me they’d let me squeeze in under the umbrella. But none of them turned round.

“I don’t know, but it was so cold!” Nia said. “It felt just like it did when we were in the Alps.” She turned her head and spotted me. “Oh, hi, Anna,” she said.

"Hi, Nia. That sounds amazing!" I said.

She smiled. No one moved to make space for me. I felt really awkward just standing there with rain dripping off my nose.

"Did you have a nice weekend, Shavina?" said Nia.

"Yeah, it was OK," said Shavina. "I had a county competition. I won the freestyle, but we lost the relay."

Shavina was a brilliant swimmer and spent so much time in water that I was surprised she hadn't turned into a fish.

"I went to my street-dance club!" said Erin. "It was so cool. We're doing a routine at the school fete next weekend!"

The three girls all smiled.

"Oh, that's great, Erin!" said Shavina.

“How about you, Anna?” said Nia. “Did you do anything nice at the weekend?”

I opened my mouth. I had nothing to say. I didn’t do anything out of school and my mind was a total blank. Nia, Shavina and Erin all watched me, waiting for me to say something. Our teacher, Miss Burnell, suddenly called out across the playground.

“Come on in out of the rain, Badgers Class!” she said.

I closed my mouth. I was saved.

Chapter Two

We headed inside to our classroom. The windows began to steam up as we took off our wet coats and brushed the rainwater from our school uniforms.

Erin and I shared a desk with Anthony and Seb. I sat down next to her and she smiled at me. Erin's hair was damp and frizzy, and she began to weave it into a braid. It looked lovely.

"Your street-dance club sounds great, Erin," I said.

"You should come, Anna. You'd love it!" said Erin.

I smiled and nodded, but that was never going to happen. We'd all been given a flyer about the new club starting in the community centre a couple of months ago. Erin and a few of the boys had signed up right away. Those kinds of clubs were really expensive, so I hadn't bothered to ask my parents.

Miss Burnell placed a cardboard box on top of her desk.

"What's that, Miss?" said Erin. "Have you been shopping online?" Erin always talked to teachers like they were someone from her family or a friend.

"I'm going to show you in just a minute, Erin," said Miss Burnell. Her eyes twinkled. Then the bell went, signalling that school had begun. She waited for everyone to settle down and then she stood up.

"OK, Badgers Class," said Miss Burnell. "Before I take the register this morning I have some special news. I'm very excited to say that we have a new student joining our class today."

We looked around the room, trying to spot where they were, but there were no new faces.

"This student is very special because they aren't able to come to school in person," said Miss Burnell. "They have an illness which means they need to stay at home so that they won't come into contact with any germs."

Anthony's hand shot up. Miss Burnell ignored him.

"They attended another school but just moved to this area," Miss Burnell went on. "I'm sure you can imagine how daunting it must be to join a new class. I hope you'll make them feel very welcome."

Anthony stretched his arm even higher. Miss Burnell nodded at him.

"How are they going to join our class if they can't come to school?" Anthony said.

Miss Burnell smiled. "I'll show you," she said. She reached into the cardboard box and took out a large white object. There was a hushed gasp as she turned it around.

"It's a robot!" said Erin.

It had a big white cube for a body and a smaller cube for its head. On the small cube were two oval shapes that looked like eyes.

"This is how our new pupil attended her previous school," Miss Burnell explained. "The robot is connected to her tablet at home, so she will be able to see and hear what we're doing in class. It'll be as if she were here with us. Isn't that clever?"

Miss Burnell pressed something on the bottom of the robot and the top of the white cube head lit up blue and its eyes glowed white. On the bottom cube were a few holes close together that looked like some kind of speaker.

"Woah!" said Seb. "It's waking up!"

There were two strips of lights on the sides of the robot which blinked steadily for a few moments, then went solid.

"I think we'll position the robot here, next to Billy," said Miss Burnell.

Billy stared at the robot and leaned away from it.

"Miss! You can put it next to me if you want to?" said Nia from the back of the class.

"Thank you, Nia, but it needs to be at the front so that the camera has a clear view of the lesson," said Miss Burnell. She went back to her desk.

"OK. I'm going to take the register now," she said.

We'd heard the register so many times we knew exactly when our names were. We all waited to see what would happen when a new name was called.

"Bea," Miss Burnell began.

"Yes, Miss."

"Katie."

"Yes, Miss."

"Nia."

"Yes, Miss."

"Anna."

"Yes, Miss," I said.

"David."

"Yes, Miss."

"Ellie."

We all froze. There wasn't an Ellie in our class. Well, not yet, anyway.

Everyone stared at the robot. The top of its head glowed blue and the white eyes wiggled up and down. And then a tiny voice came from inside the robot.

"Yes, Miss," it said.

Chapter Three

After the register, Miss Burnell began our first lesson. Everyone in the class kept looking over at the robot to see what it was doing.

Miss Burnell was busy writing some fractions onto the whiteboard and Erin leaned towards me. "What do you think is wrong with her?" Erin whispered.

"Who?" I said.

"Ellie!" said Erin. "It must be serious if she's too sick to be at school for so long."

I just shrugged.

"I might ask my mum if I can have a robot," said Seb, slumping back in his chair. "I can play on the Xbox and be at school at the same time."

Erin and Anthony laughed.

"OK, Badgers," said Miss Burnell. She turned to face us. "Who would like to solve the first equation on the board?"

Suddenly we heard a whirl and the robot's head turned to the left. Everyone gasped.

"Miss! It moved!" yelled Billy.

"Yes," said Miss Burnell. "Ellie can control the robot from her home so that she can see everything that's going on in the classroom."

The head of the robot slowly turned to the right and then back to the centre again.

"Ellie?" Miss Burnell said. "Would you like to show the class what else the robot can do?"

"Um, OK," said Ellie, through the robot.

Miss Burnell turned the robot around so everyone could see. A light at the top of the head began to flash blue.

"This means I want to ask a question," said Ellie.

"Oh, wow!" said Erin.

"And this is when I don't understand something," said Ellie. The eyes of the robot moved left and right, looking confused.

"This is when I'm happy," said Ellie. The robot's eyes looked like large letter As and wiggled.

"And this is when I'm sad," said Ellie. The eyes on the robot drooped as if they were half closed.

"That robot is well cool," said Seb.

"I was thinking we should come up with a better name than 'robot'," Miss Burnell said. "Don't you, Badgers? Is that OK, Ellie?"

The eyes on the robot went back to normal.

"Sure!" said Ellie.

Anthony's hand shot up. "How about Ellie-bot?" he said.

Miss Burnell laughed and the eyes on the robot began to wiggle, showing that Ellie was happy.

"It looks as if Ellie likes that," said Miss Burnell. "Ellie-bot it is! Right. Back to Maths."

She turned back to the whiteboard and we carried on with our lesson.

*

It was surprising how quickly we got used to having Ellie-bot in the classroom. We all stared at it the first couple of times the top of its head flashed blue and Ellie asked a question. But after that it became normal. It felt like Ellie was really there with us.

At break-time Miss Burnell asked if she could have a chat with me.

"Anna," she said. "I'd like you to partner up with Ellie-bot."

I was confused. How could I partner up with a robot?

"Me? But how?" I asked.

"I want you to be Ellie's go-to person for any questions she might have about school life," said Miss Burnell. "I'm sure she'd like to hear from a student. You can tell her all about yourself and what you like doing in and out of school."

I stared at Miss Burnell's desk. I didn't do *anything* out of school. Nia would have been a far better person to do it. Nia was super-confident and her life was so busy with all her hobbies. What would I have to talk about?

I looked over at the desk where Ellie-bot was still sitting.

"Can you ask someone else, Miss?" I whispered. I didn't want Ellie to hear me.

Miss Burnell shook her head. "I would really like it to be you, Anna. OK?"

I knew that she'd made her mind up and I didn't have a choice. Teachers are good at that: making it sound as if you've agreed to do something you don't want to do.

"All right," I said. "What do I have to do?"

I could hear everyone laughing and running outside. It wasn't raining now and the sun was shining. Nia, Shavina and Erin would be in the top playground talking. I'd normally be there too, even if I did more listening than chatting.

"Just start by introducing yourself," Miss Burnell said. "How does that sound?"

I sighed. I didn't know Ellie and I was expected to chat with her through a robot. *And* she was really ill. What was I supposed to say? This would be so easy for Nia. I was about to try to get out of it again when Miss Burnell went over to the robot.

"Ellie? Are you there?" she said.

There was a pause and then a small voice replied, "Yes, Miss, I'm here."

Miss Burnell beckoned for me to come over. She pulled out the seat where Ellie would have sat if she was actually in class.

"I want to introduce you to one of the pupils in my class," said Miss Burnell. She turned the robot around so it was staring right at me. "This is Anna and she's going to tell you a little bit about herself and our school."

Miss Burnell gave me a smile.

"I'll leave you two to it," she said. She picked up our English books and headed out of the classroom.

Chapter Four

I stared at the robot and felt my face go pink. It seemed like the robot was staring at me.

"Um. I guess I'll just start with … hello," I said. "I'm Anna." I felt so awkward it was unreal.

Nothing happened for a moment and then the robot's white eyes began to wiggle up and down. She was saying she was happy.

"Hello, Anna," said Ellie. "Sorry you've got stuck inside with me at break-time."

I smiled. “Oh, that’s fine,” I said. “I don’t do much at break-time anyway.” I wasn’t sure if that sounded a bit rude, but the robot’s eyes did another wiggle. I laughed.

“Do you like school?” said Ellie.

“It’s all right,” I said. “Miss Burnell is really nice.”

The robot hummed on the desk. Its eyes stayed in the happy setting. I sat there silent, trying to think of what I could say.

“Did you go to school before … um … before you got … ill?” I said. I instantly wished I hadn’t mentioned Ellie’s illness. That was probably the last thing she wanted to talk about! But Ellie didn’t seem to mind.

“Yes, but I haven’t been to school in person for about a year now,” she said.

I nodded. We sat in silence for a bit. I didn't know what else to say.

"Where do you sit, Anna? Do you want to show me?" said Ellie.

"Sure!" I said. I carefully twisted the robot round so that it faced my empty desk. "I sit over there on the left with Erin, Seb and Anthony."

I turned the robot back to face me again.

"I could show you around the rest of the classroom if you want?" I said.

The eyes on the robot wiggled again.

"Yes, please!" said Ellie. "You can tell me where everyone sits and what they're like!"

I grinned, then carefully picked up the robot. I turned it round so that I was holding it against my chest, its eyes facing outwards.

"OK, so let's start with Miss Burnell's desk," I said. I pointed the robot at the shelf behind her chair. "She keeps all of our workbooks here and she puts the book she's currently reading on this stand so that we can see what it is."

"Oh, I love reading. Don't you?" said Ellie.

I thought about it. Did I like reading? I hadn't read a book in ages.

"It's OK, I guess," I said.

I walked slowly around the class, showing Ellie where everyone sat. Then I went to the back wall where there was a big display of our latest art work. We had used pastels and chalks to draw Bronze Age tools.

"They look amazing!" said Ellie. "Which one is yours?"

I had to search for it. I'd never looked for my picture, but it had to be somewhere on the wall.

“There it is,” I said. It was right in the centre. It had been pretty hard to do because you couldn’t rub the pastel out if you went wrong.

“That’s brilliant, Anna!” said Ellie. “It’s the best one on the wall, for sure.”

I hadn’t noticed, but maybe she was right: it actually looked quite good.

I turned away from the display. I wasn't sure what else to show her. I think Ellie could tell I was struggling, as she started talking.

"What kind of things do you like doing out of school, Anna?" said Ellie.

My mind was blank.

I sat down in Nia's seat, which was at the back of the class, and placed Ellie-bot on her desk.

"I watch TV," I said. It sounded stupid, but I couldn't think of anything else. The only thing we did as a family was to go on picnics. That didn't cost anything.

"I like TV too," said Ellie.

I thought I should ask Ellie what she liked doing, but I was a bit worried that she might be too poorly to do anything. I didn't want to upset her. I smiled awkwardly at the robot.

"Is there anything else you like?" I said. "Apart from watching TV?"

Ellie-bot's eyes danced again.

"Oh, yes!" Ellie said. "I like baking. Shortbread, muffins and cupcakes are my favourites. I'm also learning lots about the *Titanic* at the moment. I *love* history so much. I'd like to be a historian one day."

I wondered if Ellie was smiling. Her voice sounded bright and happy.

"That sounds great," I said.

"I also like birdwatching," said Ellie. "We've got lots of bird feeders in our garden, so sometimes I sit and write down all the birds that I see. Oh, and I like making jewellery. I'm making some bracelets at the moment and—"

"Oh. Hi, Anna," said a voice.

I looked up. It was Nia. She came over and picked up her water bottle. She must have forgotten it.

"I'm just showing Ellie around the classroom," I said.

Nia crouched down beside me.

"We were just talking about our hobbies," said Ellie.

Nia grinned. "Great!" she said. "You should see our 'Interests Board'! Have you shown her, Anna?" Nia looked at me.

I shook my head. Why hadn't I thought of that?

Nia grabbed the robot and walked off to the corner of the classroom. Miss Burnell had created a space for us to share the activities that we did out of school.

"This is me at ballet," said Nia. She held the robot in front of a photo of her in a white leotard. The picture next to it was another one of Nia. This time she was sitting on a chestnut-coloured horse. "And here I am with Pumpkin," she said.

"Oh, wow! Have you got your own horse?" said Ellie.

"Yes!" Nia said. "He's such a soppy thing. You'd love him! I'm going to the stables after school today."

Ellie giggled. Nia made it look so easy. They sounded like best friends already.

The robot's head slowly moved up and down as Ellie looked around the board.

"There's Anthony playing football," Nia said. "His team won the league and he got a cup. And there's Beatrice doing trampolining. Oh, and there's another one of me, playing the piano."

I hovered by the board feeling more and more awkward.

"Wow," said Ellie. "You sure are busy, Nia. Are you on there, Anna?"

I swallowed. I had one photograph on the "Interests Board".

"Yep. I'm in the top corner," I said.

Nia lifted Ellie-bot up to the picture of me, Dad, Mum and Henry having a picnic.

"Oh, that's lovely," said Ellie. "I love being outdoors and watching nature."

It felt a bit like she was just trying to be polite.

"Oh look, there's Erin at her street-dance club," said Nia. She stopped by a photograph of Erin wearing a black hoodie and grey sweatpants. "Are you coming to the school fete on Saturday, Ellie? Erin's club are performing."

Ellie-bot's eyes drooped. "No. I won't be able to," she said quietly.

"Oh, that's a shame," said Nia. "Anna and I are running a stall. You could have helped too."

None of us spoke for a moment. I was trying to think what I could say to make Ellie feel better for not coming to the fete.

"Hey, Ellie. Would you like to see the library now?" I said to the tiny round camera.

Nia scrunched up her nose.

"The library?" she said. "I'm sure you'd rather see something a bit more exciting, wouldn't you, Ellie?" She turned Ellie-bot so that the camera faced her.

"I don't mind," said Ellie softly.

“Great!” said Nia. “We’ll go on a tour! You’re going to *love* it. Let me take you to find Shavina and Erin. You don’t mind, do you, Anna?”

I shook my head and Nia skipped off across the classroom and the door closed behind her.

I went over to my desk and sat down.

It was probably for the best. Miss Burnell should have chosen Nia to look after Ellie in the first place. But thinking that didn't stop the feeling I had inside. I felt like I was deflating, just like a burst balloon. All of the air seeped out until I was very, very small indeed.

Chapter Five

At exactly three o'clock I looked out of the window and saw that it had begun to rain again. Sometimes I thought the weather knew just when school started and finished. Twenty minutes later we were packing our things away, getting ready to go home.

"Before you go, Badgers Class, I want to tell you something," Miss Burnell said. "I'm going to change the seating around tomorrow."

A few people groaned and a few more said "*Yes!*" under their breath.

"When you come in tomorrow morning," Miss Burnell said, "please look for where I've placed your English books. That will be your new seat until the end of term."

Miss Burnell was one of those teachers who liked to "mix it up a bit" and move the classroom around. I'd been sitting at the same desk for the past month and I liked it there. I didn't like it when we changed around. I worried about who I'd end up next to.

*

When I got out of school, I headed up the hill to where Mum normally parked. Henry was asleep in the back of the car. Nursery always wore him out.

"Hey, Anna," said Mum. "All ready for the supermarket?"

I huffed. I'd forgotten about that. "I guess," I said.

We drove down the road, passing Shavina and Erin and some others from my class. They were probably all going off to do their exciting clubs or hobbies. A knot of envy twisted deep inside my stomach.

"How was school, Anna?" said Mum.

"Fine. We had a new girl start today," I said.

"Ah. Is she nice?" said Mum.

"Yes, I think so," I said. "She's not very well, so she has to stay at home and watch the lessons through this cool robot. She's called Ellie."

"Oh, yes, I've heard about Ellie," said Mum. "The school sent out an email explaining how it's all going to work. It sounds so clever."

Mum checked her mirror before she turned a corner.

"Do you know what is wrong with her?" I said. "What I mean is ... is it serious?"

We pulled up to a roundabout and stopped to let a bus go past. We followed the bus, then turned off down the road where the supermarket was.

"I don't know exactly," Mum said, "but the email mentioned that she's finished her treatment. I think the important thing has been to keep her away from any risk of catching germs, in case they make her really poorly."

I hoped Ellie was going to be OK.

"Miss Burnell asked me to look after her at break-time," I said. "But I don't think I did it very well."

"What do you mean?" said Mum.

I couldn't say that it was because everyone else was far more interesting than me as they actually did things out of school. If I said that, Mum might feel bad.

"Oh, you know, it's just awkward talking to a robot," I said.

Mum was frowning as she looked left and right for a parking space. It was hard to get parked at the supermarket sometimes.

"Ha! Look," Mum said. "There's a space! Excellent!" She put the indicator on and pulled into a gap between two white cars.

Mum turned to face me.

"Just be yourself, Anna," she said. "That's always good enough. OK?"

I nodded. It didn't sound good enough to me.

"Come on," Mum said. "Let's wake your brother up and get shopping, shall we?" She had a huge smile on her face. I sighed and climbed out of the car into the pouring rain. I couldn't see much to be so cheerful about.

Chapter Six

The supermarket was fine until Henry got his finger trapped in the bars of the trolley. His cries were so loud you'd have thought he was having his arm sawn off. Everyone was staring at us. Mum took him out of the seat and carried him around, blowing raspberries on his cheek. Before long, Henry had forgotten all about his finger and was in fits of laughter. Mum was good at distractions.

When we got home, Dad was at the door to help with the shopping. Henry trotted up the path and Dad scooped him up under one arm.

“Ah, and where does this bag of shopping go, I wonder?” he said.

Henry started giggling and kicking his legs under Dad’s arm as Dad walked into the kitchen with him. I followed them and Dad gave Henry a big kiss on his cheek before putting him down. Dad began to butter a slice of toast. He worked nights as a security guard and so he had his breakfast when we were thinking about dinner. He slept during the daytime.

“Nice day, Anna?” Dad said.

“Yes, fine,” I said. “I’m going to go and do my homework.”

I went up to my room. On my desk was a collage that I’d started about a month ago. I’d seen a post online from a girl who had made one and put it on her wall. I thought it looked amazing, so I had a go at doing my own version.

I'd found a large piece of paper and drew the outline of a heart in pencil. I then cut out pieces of coloured paper from some old magazines that we had in the house into small petal shapes. Then I dabbed some glue at one end and layered

the petals like feathers in the giant heart shape. I'd been trying to blend the colours so that it looked like the heart was fading around the edges, but I had only got about halfway.

I remembered the day when I'd stopped. During break-time the girls in class had been talking about going go-karting one Saturday. I hadn't said anything, knowing it wasn't something I'd be allowed to do. I'd got home that day and my picture had suddenly felt pointless. I'd just given up. I sighed and propped it against the wall so I had room to do my homework.

*

When I walked into class the next day, I heard a mixture of moans and cheers as everyone found out who they were sitting with for the next few weeks. Erin and Shavina were screeching and hugging each other as they'd discovered they were on the same desk.

Ellie-bot was sitting on a desk at the front. I looked at one of the English books beside the robot and read the name:

ANNA HIGSON

It was mine! I felt a fizz of happiness deep in my stomach when I sat down. The two strips of white lights on the robot's sides were lit, so I knew it was turned on. The head of the robot slowly swivelled to face me.

"Hi, Anna!" said Ellie.

"Hi, Ellie," I said. I gave her a smile and the robot's head flashed and its eyes did a jiggle. I laughed, but then someone pushed the back of my seat and I was jolted forwards.

"Sorry, Anna. Can I get past?" said a voice.

I looked round. It was Nia. I edged my chair in and looked over at the English book on the other side of Ellie-bot. It was Nia's. Yes, she was my friend, but my heart still sank a bit.

"Oh, hi, Ellie!" said Nia brightly.

"Hi, Nia," said Ellie back, but the robot didn't flash or wiggle its eyes. "How is Pumpkin?" said Ellie. "Did you ride him last night?"

"Yes!" said Nia. "I've been teaching him how to jump and he is just beginning to get the hang of it. He's such a star."

Fortunately, I didn't have to listen to any more of Nia's exciting life, as Miss Burnell began to take the register. When she'd finished, she asked Nia to go to the school office to collect some photocopying that she'd left behind. The rest of us were told to turn to a fresh page in our English books while Miss Burnell handed out copies of a poem.

"How was yesterday, Anna?" said Ellie. "Did you do anything nice after school?"

Ellie-bot turned its head to face me. I thought about last night. Of me, Mum and Henry going to the supermarket and then coming home to dinner. It wasn't exactly exciting for her to hear about that. I blinked a few times, then smiled at the robot.

"My mum picked me up after school and we went to the new ice-cream parlour in town with my little brother," I said. As soon as the words left my lips, I regretted it. What was I doing?!

"Oh, how lovely!" said Ellie. "I've heard it's really nice there. What flavour ice cream did you have?" She sounded so interested, I had to carry on.

"I had a chocolate sundae," I said. "With an extra flake and toffee sauce." I had never been to the ice-cream parlour before, but as I spoke I could almost picture us there, sitting in one of the booths with the bright red padded seats.

"Henry had a strawberry sundae and it was so tall he had to kneel on his seat to eat it!" I said. I imagined me and Henry laughing and sharing a scoop of each other's ice creams.

"That sounds like a lot of fun," said Ellie. "Did you do anything else?"

I should have stopped right there, but it was too tempting to keep going. I was enjoying saying that I'd actually done something for once, even if it wasn't true.

"After the ice creams, we met up with my dad and we all went ten-pin bowling," I said. "Henry is only two, so he just watched and had a go at pushing the ball down the ramp now and then."

This part of my story was true, but it had happened about ten months ago. Mum had won a family ticket to go bowling in a raffle in the office where she worked. I didn't think there was any harm in adding the story in now.

“Great!” said Ellie. “I love ten-pin bowling.”

I grinned. “Me too!” I said. “And after that we went to the American diner and got hamburgers.”

Ellie was quiet for a moment.

“Wow, that’s a lot of things,” she said. “Was it someone’s birthday?”

I bit my bottom lip. She was right. It was a lot of things to do on a regular Monday afternoon. I’d definitely overdone it.

“No,” I said. “Dad got a pay rise at work and ... um ... he thought he’d treat us. We don’t normally have that much fun!” I did a little laugh.

“Well, it sounds like a wonderful evening,” said Ellie. The head of the robot turned and faced the front.

I swallowed. I felt awful for lying, but I also wanted Ellie to like me. My life was not interesting. If I didn't make something up, then what would we have to talk about? Surely there wasn't any harm in that?

Chapter Seven

Ellie was great to sit next to in class. At first, I wondered if she might have a hard time keeping up, as she'd missed so much school. But Ellie was really clever and the light on top of Ellie-bot often flashed blue, which meant she wanted to answer a question. She told me that her mum had picked up all the books and printouts that she would need for this week's lessons. Ellie had already become just another pupil in Badgers Class.

The last lesson of the day was science. We'd been learning about the digestive system and Miss Burnell told us to work in groups of three and gave us a printed diagram of the insides of the abdomen. We had to label all the parts. Ellie, Nia and I set to work and we'd finished it within minutes.

Nia leaned on her elbow and smiled at Ellie-bot.

"It's such a shame you can't come to the school fete on Saturday, Ellie," said Nia.

The eyes of Ellie-bot wiggled. "I forgot to tell you!" said Ellie. "Mum said that Miss Burnell is going to take Ellie-bot along. So I can be there after all! Maybe not in person, but it's the next best thing. Can I help on your stall?"

"Of course you can!" said Nia. "We're in charge of the Hook-A-Duck game."

"That's great, Ellie!" I said.

*

At the end of the day we handed in our work and began to pack our things away.

"Are you riding your horse again tonight, Nia?" said Ellie.

"No," said Nia. "I've got a French class straight after school and then a piano lesson."

Nia zipped up her pencil case and threw it into her bag.

"My parents are keen for me to learn a second language and an instrument," Nia said. "They think it'll look good when I apply for university later on." She pressed her lips together and smiled.

"OK, Badgers," said Miss Burnell. "When you've cleared your desks, you're free to go."

"Bye, Anna. Bye, Ellie," said Nia. "See you in the morning!"

She threw her bag over her shoulder and rushed off. I knew that on Tuesdays Nia's mum would be waiting outside in the car with the engine running.

I put my books into my rucksack and Ellie-bot twisted round to face me.

"Thanks for working with me today, Anna," said Ellie.

"That's all right," I said. "I'm glad you're helping on the stall on Saturday. It should be fun!"

"Yes! I'm looking forward to it," said Ellie. "And how about you? Are you doing anything nice tonight like Nia?"

I paused for a moment. I knew exactly what I would be doing tonight. Nothing.

I looked at Ellie-bot as she waited for me to answer.

"On Tuesdays I go ... ice skating," I said. It was the first thing that popped into my head.

"Oh, wow! Are you having lessons?" said Ellie.

I nodded. "Yep," I said.

"You must be good!" Ellie said. "I went once and I couldn't let go of the side!" She laughed.

I smiled. That was the same as me! I'd gone ice skating for Erin's birthday last year and I could barely stand up.

"I guess you must have your own skates?" said Ellie.

"Yes! White ones," I said. I could almost picture the shiny white skates with twinkling silver blades sitting in the bottom of my wardrobe.

“I hope it goes well,” Ellie said. “You can tell me all about it tomorrow! Bye, Anna!”

“Bye, Ellie,” I gulped back. The lights on the robot flickered off.

I picked up my bag and headed out to meet Mum.

Chapter Eight

I sat at my desk the next morning and saw that Ellie-bot was already switched on. Nia was by the coat pegs chatting to Shavina.

"Hi, Ellie," I said to the robot. "How are you?"

"I'm fine," said Ellie. "How was ice skating?"

I looked over at Nia. She was still talking, but I had to be quick.

"It was great!" I said. "We're learning how to skate backwards."

"Oh, wow. I bet that's hard!" said Ellie.

I nodded and clammed up as Nia walked behind me to get to her seat. She knew I didn't go ice skating, so I couldn't let her hear. I could feel my cheeks beginning to burn red with the lie, so I bent down and pretended to get something out of my bag. Miss Burnell started taking the register and we all had to turn to face the front.

*

I spent the rest of the week telling Ellie even more lies. As well as ten-pin bowling and ice skating, I told Ellie that I had been trampolining and gone to football training. I hadn't done any of those things, but the more I lied, the easier it became. I suddenly had so much to say that the words just flowed. And Ellie seemed to like hearing about it too.

On Friday, Ellie was really quiet and didn't contribute much to class. Nia and I had both asked if anything was wrong, but Ellie kept saying that she was fine. Ellie-bot's eyes looked sad, though, and I wondered if she had something on her mind.

Before the end of the day, Nia tried to cheer Ellie up by talking about the school fete.

"We'll take you round all the stalls tomorrow," Nia said. "That way you can see everything that goes on. Won't we, Anna?"

I nodded. "Yes! It'll be just as good as being there," I said.

"Thank you," said Ellie, but her voice sounded very flat. As soon as Miss Burnell said we could leave for the day, the lights of the robot turned off before we got a chance to say goodbye.

Chapter Nine

The next day was Saturday and Mum dropped me at school early so that I could help set up our stall for the summer fete.

Nia was already on the school field dressed in denim shorts and a T-shirt. For our stall we had a table and two chairs, and a deflated yellow paddling pool on the grass. There was also a foot pump, a clear plastic bag full of bright orange ducks and two sticks with golden hooks.

"Hi, Anna," said Nia.

“Hi,” I said. “Shall I pump up the paddling pool?”

Nia flopped onto one of the chairs.

“Oh, yes, that would be brilliant,” she said.

I fixed the end of the tube into the small valve on the pool and began to press my foot up and down on the pump. I looked at Nia as she sorted through a tub of sweets. She looked exhausted and she had dark rings under her eyes.

“Are you feeling OK, Nia?” I said.

She nodded.

“Yes. I’m just really tired,” she said. “I got back late from ballet last night and was up early to come here. I’m off to the stables after this.”

I watched Nia as the paddling pool slowly inflated. She really didn’t look happy at all.

Maybe being so active wasn't always such a good thing? When I thought about it, I wondered if she ever had any down time.

Miss Burnell came over carrying Ellie-bot in one arm and a bucket in the other. The robot was glowing blue and she placed it on the table.

"Hi, Anna! Hi, Nia!" called Ellie. I was pleased to hear her sound much brighter today.

"Hi!" Nia and I said back. I pulled the pump tube out of the pool and pushed the stopper in.

"Right, it's ready for the water now, Miss," I said.

"Great!" said Miss Burnell. "Just fill it up with the bucket using the tap in the staff toilet. Have you got everything else that you need?"

"Yep, we're all sorted," said Nia, perking up.

"Wonderful. I'll catch up with you three later," Miss Burnell said, and headed off to help Seb and Anthony with the tombola.

"We can take it in turns getting the water if you like?" said Nia.

"It's OK," I said. "You're tired. I can do it."

Nia smiled at me and I headed off with the bucket.

It only took seven buckets to fill the small pool. We dropped the bag of ducks into the water and watched as they bobbed around.

"I know! I can be in charge of finding customers!" said Ellie. "How about this? Roll-up! Roll-up! Come and hook a duck and win some fabulous prizes!" Her voice boomed out of the robot.

Nia and I laughed. Ellie was so nice. I wished she could be here with us, but having Ellie-bot was the next best thing.

*

The school fete was a huge success. The sun shone and everyone who came along was in a really good mood. Our stall was busy, especially when families realised the famous "Ellie-bot" was working there. In fact, I think having Ellie there made us the most popular stall in the fete.

Mum came along with Henry and he managed to hook three ducks to win some sweets. I'd had such a wonderful morning that it made what happened next even more upsetting. We began to pack our stall away and things suddenly turned bad.

Chapter Ten

It all went wrong because of the paddling pool. I was busy with the bucket, scooping out the water and sloshing it onto the grass. Shavina and Erin came over. They had been running a stall where you had to knock cans over using small beanbags.

"Hi, guys!" said Shavina.

"Hi, Ellie," said Erin. She was wearing her tracksuit from her street-dance club.

"Hi!" said Ellie. "Your dance was brilliant, Erin." Erin's street-dance club had performed a routine in the middle of the field and we'd taken Ellie-bot closer to watch.

Erin smiled. "Thanks!" she said. "How did your stall go?"

Nia tipped out a pile of coins from a plastic tub. "It was great," she said. "Mainly thanks to Ellie-bot, who was so good at calling in the crowds."

Ellie-bot's eyes wiggled and flashed, and we all laughed.

The paddling pool was nearly empty, so I lifted one side and the water gushed out onto the grass. I twisted the pool to get the last few centimetres of water out and Ellie-bot's head turned to watch.

"Oooh, look, Anna!" said Ellie. "The pool looks just like a skating rink!"

I froze. I looked at the bottom of the paddling pool which was shiny and white.

"Yes, yes, it does a bit," I said. I turned away and undid the stopper on the side to let the air out. The pool slowly began to shrink.

"Anna?" said Ellie. "I was thinking that maybe I could ask my mum if I could come and see you skate one day. Do you think your coach would let me?"

I looked down at the deflating paddling pool, then turned to face Ellie-bot. Nia, Shavina and Erin were all staring at me.

Nia was frowning. "I didn't know you did ice skating, Anna?" said Nia.

Erin took a step forwards, her arms folded. My mind raced as I tried to think of what to say. I pressed my lips together.

"You must have to travel for miles," said Shavina. "The rink just outside town closed down a while ago."

I swallowed. I didn't know that. And even if the rink was still open, there was no way that anyone would believe I was having lessons. My friends knew my family couldn't afford for me to go to any clubs.

I had two choices. I could say that I did go skating but hadn't told anyone about it, or I could deny it and say that Ellie was wrong. I had just one choice.

I smiled at Ellie-bot and felt my face stretch tightly.

"You must have misunderstood, Ellie," I said firmly. "I don't take ice-skating lessons."

There was a moment when we all went silent. The eyes on Ellie-bot moved left and right to show that she was confused.

“But you said you had lessons?” said Ellie. “You said that you had your own skates and that you’d been learning how to ice skate backwards?”

Nia frowned at me.

“Anna?” she said. “Have you been lying to Ellie?”

All four of them were waiting for me to explain. I took a few deep breaths and then suddenly Mum and Henry were there. Henry was in Mum's arms, his head resting on her shoulder. He looked exhausted.

"Hi, girls!" said Mum.

Nia, Shavina and Erin all mumbled hello. Mum turned to me.

"We need to head home now, Anna," said Mum. "Henry needs a nap."

"OK," I said. I dropped the paddling pool into a heap on the grass and muttered "Bye". I couldn't look at my friends, as I didn't want to see the disappointment and anger on their faces. I'd just ruined everything and there was nothing I could do about it.

I walked across the field with my family, feeling smaller and smaller with every step.

Chapter Eleven

I didn't speak as we drove home. Mum asked if I was OK and I said I was just tired and everything was fine. I sat in the back with Henry, who was yawning but trying to stay awake. He'd won a small plastic tractor at one of the stalls and I watched him as he rolled it up and down his leg. It was such a basic toy, but he was utterly absorbed.

"That Ellie-bot is brilliant, isn't it?" said Mum. "And Ellie seems like a really lovely girl. Miss Burnell said she's got an appointment at the hospital on Monday to see her specialist.

I got the impression it's to find out how well the treatment has been working."

I felt a tightness in my chest. *That* was probably why Ellie had been so quiet in school yesterday. She had been worried about her appointment! She'd cheered up during the fete, but I'd gone and ruined it by lying about ice skating. I wished there was some way that I could talk to Ellie.

"Mum? Do you have Ellie's mum's phone number?" I asked.

We turned left at a roundabout in the direction of home.

"No, I don't, love. I'm sorry," said Mum. She glanced at me in the rear-view mirror. "Is everything OK, Anna?"

A large lump had formed in my throat.

"Yes," I said. "I just wanted to wish Ellie good luck for Monday and ... and ... to say that I'm sorry."

My voice cracked and I felt warm tears seep out of the corner of my eyes. Mum pulled over and we parked in a layby.

"Anna?" said Mum, turning around. "What's happened?"

It took me a while to start, but once I began to tell Mum, I couldn't stop. I told her about all the things I'd made up and that Ellie now knew everything had been a lie. It was strange, but admitting to what I'd done felt like a huge relief.

"Oh, Anna," said Mum.

I could see disappointment in her eyes. I looked down at my lap.

"I didn't get a chance to explain to Ellie why I made those things up," I said. "I didn't know she had a hospital appointment. She must be really worried about that. And now I've ruined everything!"

Mum twisted around.

"And why did you lie, Anna?" she said. "Why did you make up those things?"

I kept my eyes down. I knew I'd start sobbing if I looked at Mum.

"I guess I just wanted to be like everybody else," I said. "I wanted Ellie to think I was interesting and that I have a life."

Henry stopped rolling the tractor along his thigh and stared at me. I think he must have sensed something was going on, even if he was too young to understand what it was.

"Is that what makes someone interesting?" said Mum. "Just because of the number of clubs they go to? Or how much money they have?"

I frowned. “What do you mean?” I said.

“I mean, can’t someone be interesting without all of that?” said Mum.

I didn't say anything.

"Why do you like Ellie, Anna?" Mum said. "I'm guessing she's not able to take part in clubs right now."

I thought about it. "Ellie is different," I said. "She's funny and clever and she's really easy to talk to. She's got loads of interests like reading and making jewellery and baking."

"But you used to love reading!" said Mum. "And what about your painting and sketching? You've stopped making your beautiful pictures, Anna. Why?"

I shrugged. My head was hurting as I thought about all those things I used to do. "I guess I didn't think they were enough," I said.

Mum patted the top of my knee. "You know what, Anna?" she said. "I think that you've been so fixated on being someone you think you should be, that you've forgotten how to be *you*."

Mum smiled at me and then turned around and started the engine. We drove the rest of the way home in silence.

Chapter Twelve

On Monday I went into class with my stomach churning. The lies I had told Ellie weren't the thing that was worrying me the most. It was Ellie's hospital appointment. Was she going to be OK? Had her treatment worked?

I sat down at my desk. Nia was already in her seat and she looked up and smiled. I felt a tiny moment of relief that she was still being friendly, even after my lies. Between us there was an empty space where Ellie-bot normally sat.

"Hi, Nia," I said. Nia nodded at me but didn't say anything. She looked sad and a little bit angry.

I looked down at the desk for a few moments and then back up at her.

"Nia?" I said. "I didn't mean to lie to Ellie. I just got carried away. The rest of you all do so many activities and I just wanted to feel interesting for once. I'm sorry."

Nia took a deep breath.

"OK," she said. She chewed on her bottom lip for a moment, then looked at me. "Sometimes being so busy isn't such a good thing, you know?" Nia said.

I remembered how tired she had looked at the fete and how often her mum was waiting outside school with her car engine running, ready to dash to the next club.

I nodded.

"Are you OK?" Nia said.

She was making sure I was OK? After everything that I'd done? She *was* a good friend.

"I'm fine, thank you, Nia," I said. "I'm just sad I can't talk to Ellie to say sorry."

Nia nodded. "We all make mistakes, Anna," she said. "I'm sure Ellie will understand."

Her words made me feel a bit better, but I still kept Ellie in the front of my mind all day.

At the end of school after everyone had left, I walked over to Miss Burnell's desk and asked if there had been any news on Ellie's hospital appointment.

"No, we've not heard anything yet, Anna," she said. "I'm sure we'll find out soon."

Ellie-bot was sitting on the shelf behind Miss Burnell's desk. It was turned off, so its eyes were blank as it stared out at the empty classroom. The robot seemed so vacant without Ellie at the other end making its eyes dance and her cheerful voice coming through the speaker. Ellie was what brought the robot to life.

*

I went straight to my room when I got home. A lot had happened over the past few days and I had done a lot of thinking, especially about what Mum had said about forgetting to be me.

I sat on my bed and looked at my desk. The heart collage I'd started was still propped up against the wall. Some of the pieces were a bit wonky, but it really didn't look too bad on the whole.

Under my bed I had a small plastic tub filled with a few art materials next to a pile of old magazines. I put them all on my desk and sat down in my chair. I was going to finish it.

*

I worked on my collage right up until dinner time and then again until it was time for bed. Mum knocked on my door after Henry had gone to sleep.

"Are you all right, love?" she asked, poking her head round my door.

"Yes, I'm fine, Mum," I said. "I'll just be another five minutes and then I'll go to sleep."

She smiled when she saw what I was doing and blew me a kiss.

I stuck the last petal piece into place, then picked up my finished collage. It was a kaleidoscope of colour. I moved the paper back and forth so that the pieces began to flutter.

I smiled to myself. It looked like the heart was gently beating.

Chapter Thirteen

Mum dropped me at school the next day. I ran to the playground and stood by the main doors. As soon as the bell went, I rushed to our classroom to see if Ellie-bot was back. But the desk beside me was empty.

I felt a bit dizzy. Something bad had happened to Ellie, I just knew it. I looked for Miss Burnell to ask her what was going on, but she was in the corner talking to our headteacher, Mrs Watson.

I put my bag by my desk and sat down. Miss Burnell and Mrs Watson were talking in low whispers, looking down at the floor as they spoke. Ellie-bot was on the shelf behind them, switched off and facing the wall. Miss Burnell saw me looking and she quickly turned away. Then Miss Burnell nodded and Mrs Watson left.

Almost everyone was in their seats now. I put my arm up.

"Miss?" I said. "Miss? Is Ellie OK?"

Miss Burnell waved her arm at me. "Not now, Anna," she said. "Let me take the register and then I need to tell you something." She went over to her desk.

I felt tears begin to sting my eyes. It wasn't going to be good. I just knew it.

Miss Burnell called out everyone's names and I waited for her to get to Ellie Palmer, but she skipped it. She finished the register and Ellie wasn't mentioned at all. Miss Burnell was holding her hands in front of her.

“Badgers Class, I have some news to share about Ellie Palmer,” she began.

My stomach twisted. I was so worried about what she was going to say.

“As you know,” Miss Burnell went on, “Ellie has been very poorly over the past year. She has been in and out of hospital and has had to endure some rather nasty treatments to try to get her better again.”

The classroom was so quiet you couldn’t even hear a breath.

“Her treatment has meant that her immune system was badly affected. This meant that she has been at risk of catching an illness and getting seriously unwell. That’s why she used Ellie-bot to join our class.” Miss Burnell turned and pointed to the robot on her shelf. The sight of the robot’s back facing the class made me want to cry. I closed my eyes tightly. This was awful.

"Ellie had an appointment at the hospital yesterday to see how her immune system was coping," said Miss Burnell.

As she spoke, I heard the classroom door open, but I kept my eyes closed.

"And I'm pleased to say that Ellie's doctor has said that she can return to school part-time!" Miss Burnell continued.

I opened my eyes and blinked. *What?!*

I turned my head and saw Mrs Watson and a small girl standing in the doorway. She was wearing school uniform and she had a pale blue scarf tied around her head.

"Ellie?" I whispered.

"Come on in," said Miss Burnell, smiling. "Come and meet your classmates!"

Ellie looked around at all of our faces. She looked really nervous, but I could tell from a twinkle in her eyes that she was also excited.

Miss Burnell put a hand on Ellie's shoulder. "This is your seat right here – next to Anna and Nia," she said.

Ellie looked at both of us and smiled. "Hi, Nia. Hi, Anna," she said.

"Hi, Ellie," I said, smiling back.

Chapter Fourteen

It was lovely having Ellie at school. She still had to take it easy, as it was going to be very tiring to return to school, so at break-time we went to the library. We sat in the corner on some beanbags and the warm sun shone through the window onto our faces.

"Ellie?" I said. "I need to talk to you about what I did and why I lied to you."

Ellie frowned. "OK," she said.

"The thing is, when I started talking to you through Ellie-bot, I felt like I didn't have anything to say," I said. "All the other girls in the class do so much, but I don't do anything."

I felt like I was going to start crying. Ellie just listened.

"That's why I made it all up," I went on. "About going to the ice-cream parlour and the ten-pin bowling. And about the ice skating and football training. The truth is, I don't go to any clubs like everyone else does. My family can't afford it. I made those things up as I was worried I didn't have anything interesting to tell you."

Ellie looked down at the book she was holding, then back at me.

"Why couldn't you just be honest?" she said. "I don't care about if you can ice skate or not."

I frowned. "I guess ... I guess I just felt like everyone else was having a good time except for me," I said. "People like Nia, well ... their

lives are so ... BIG. And I just felt so ... small. I'm sorry."

Ellie took a long breath. She seemed to be thinking. "I think that some of the most important things are small," she said.

I didn't understand.

"What do you mean?" I asked.

She looked around the library.

"Look at that sun beam coming through the glass over there," she said, pointing behind me.

I turned. There was a haze of yellow light coming down from the window and making a warm orange glow on the library carpet. The other children in the library were walking through it, not noticing it was there. I looked back at Ellie.

"Or maybe a small thing could be watching a blackbird bathing in a puddle," Ellie said, "or the delicious smell you get when you mix up the ingredients for a cake, or reading something in a book that is so interesting it makes you smile. That's what I mean about the small things."

I thought I understood what she was saying. Ellie had been through a great deal and I guess she now looked at the world in a different way to the rest of us.

"I think I see," I said.

"Sometimes it's those small things that are the best," said Ellie. "We forget to enjoy them."

"But I am sorry for lying," I said.

"It doesn't matter," Ellie said. "Let's put it behind us and just enjoy today, shall we?"

I grinned as I felt a huge wave of relief wash over me. I suddenly remembered something.

"Wait there a minute!" I said.

I ran back to class. Poking out of the top of my bag was a rolled-up piece of paper. I grabbed it and headed back to the library.

"This is for you," I said, handing Ellie the piece of paper.

Ellie unrolled the sheet.

"Oh, wow, it's a heart!" she said. "It's so beautiful."

She gently ran her fingers over the collage.

"I love it, Anna," she said. "I'm going to put it straight on my bedroom wall when I get home. Thank you."

I smiled. It had been great doing some art again. I'd forgotten how relaxed it made me feel. I was definitely going to do more.

"Come on," I said. "Let's choose some books, shall we? I think there's a few about the *Titanic* in here that you might not have read."

Ellie smiled at me and she slowly stood up.

"That sounds like a brilliant idea," she said.

Author's Note

I am very lucky with my job because I get to visit lots of schools and readers all around the UK.

A few years ago, I was about to speak at an assembly in a primary school when I saw a teacher place a white robot on a seat. She came over to me and explained that this was "Lily-Bot", and the real Lily was at home, watching the assembly through her tablet.

I was astounded! I'd never seen a robot in a school before!

After my talk, “Lily-Bot” was brought over to me and I got to “meet” the Lily that was at home. It was such a wonderful experience and this encounter inspired *The Small Things*.

These robots are created by a company called No Isolation, who produce them to help children attend school who cannot be there in person for various reasons.

I want to say a big thank you to Lily and her family for talking with me about their positive experiences with an AV1 robot (the technical name for Ellie-bot!). You have been a true inspiration!

Lisa Thompson x

Our books are tested
for children and young people by
children and young people.

Thanks to everyone who consulted on
a manuscript for their time and effort in
helping us to make our books better
for our readers.